Three Kind Mice

Written by Vivian Sathre   Illustrated by Rodger Wilson

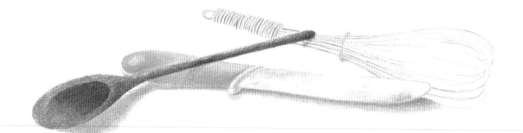

Harcourt Brace & Company

SAN DIEGO   NEW YORK   LONDON

Library of Congress Cataloging-in-Publication Data
Sathre, Vivian.
Three kind mice/written by Vivian Sathre; illustrated by Rodger Wilson.
p.   cm.
Summary: Three kind mice bake a birthday cake surprise for their mysterious friend.
ISBN 0-15-201266-4
[1. Mice—Fiction. 2. Baking—Fiction. 3. Birthdays—Fiction. 4. Stories in rhyme.]
I. Wilson, Rodger, 1947-   ill. II. Title.
PZ8.3.S238Th   1997
[E]—dc20   95-48788

First edition
A C E F D B

Printed in Mexico

The illustrations in this book were done in colored pencils on watercolor paper.
The display type was set in Fontesque by Harcourt Brace & Company
Photocomposition Center, San Diego, California.
The text type was set in Columbus by Harcourt Brace & Company
Photocomposition Center, San Diego, California.
Color separations by Bright Arts, Ltd., Singapore
Printed and bound by RR Donnelley & Sons Company, Reynosa, Mexico
This book was printed on Patina Matte paper.
Production supervision by Stanley Redfern and Ginger Boyer
Designed by Lori McThomas Buley

For three kind kids—Erika, Mitchell, and Karsten,
and three more—Julie, Jayme, and Ryan

—V. S.

For Jennie

—R. W.

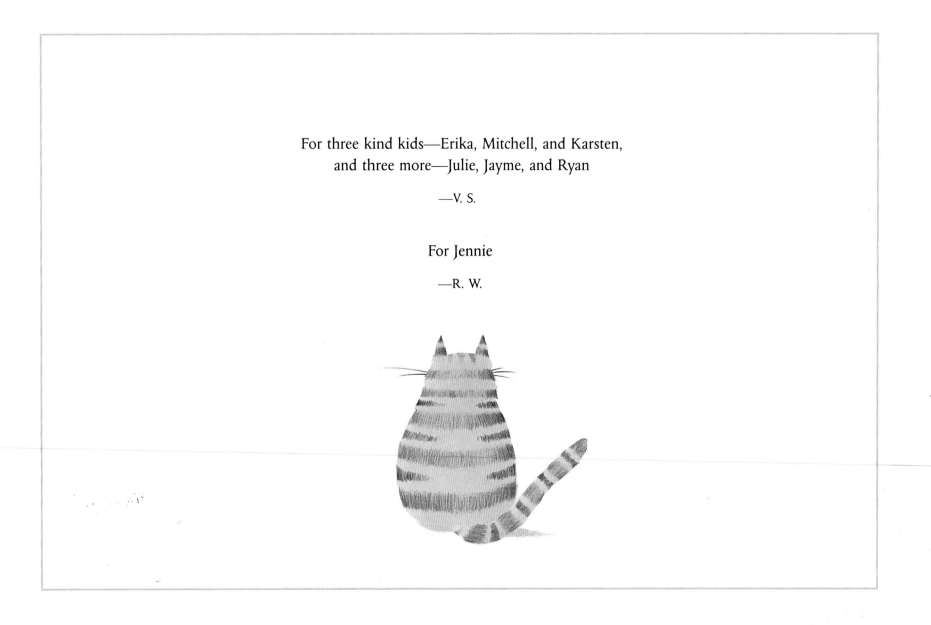

Three kind mice
mix up a cake.
Flour,
sugar,
eggs,
and milk.

Stir fast. Stir faster!
Batter spatters.

Oops! The mice fall in.
They swim.

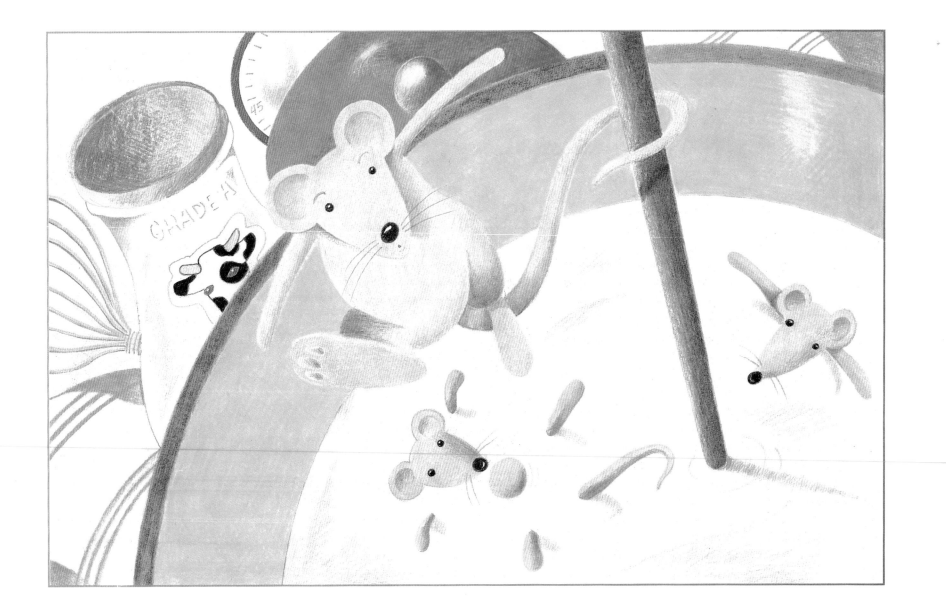

The mice climb out.
A towel appears.
Mice wipe their faces,
fluff their ears.

Mice pour the batter in a pan.

The cake bakes. The mice wait.
It's done!

The mice mix icing.
And they skate.
They swirl. They glide.
The mice collide.

Ice packs arrive
in just their size.

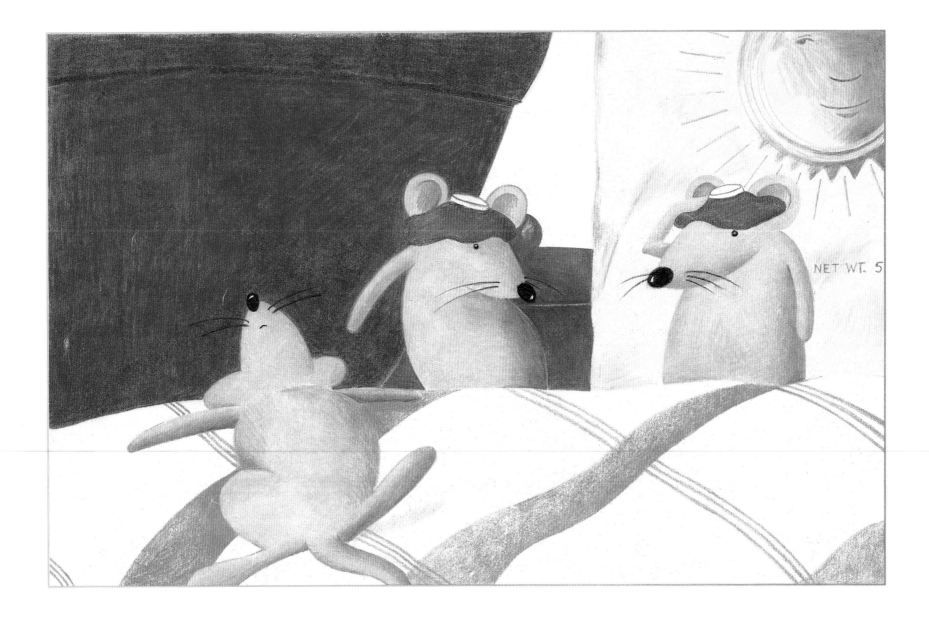

Mice eek!
They squeak.
Mice jump and shriek.
They shoo away the cat!
They slam the door.

Mice find candles.
Slide, step, poke. Slide, step, poke.

A candle falls. One mouse trips.
All three mice begin to slip—
right off the edge.

Mice take a rest.
Then they all
clean up the mess.

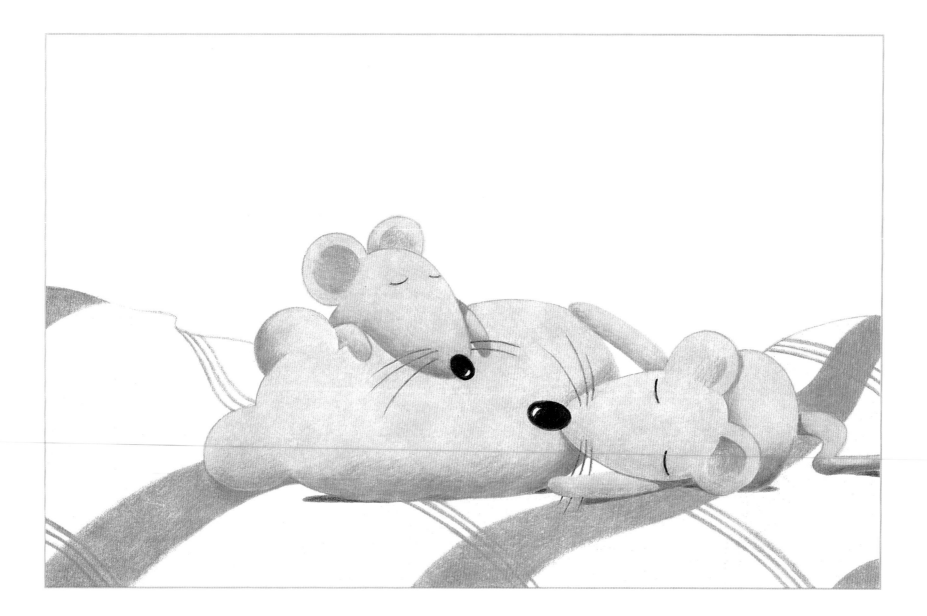

But three kind mice
have one thing left to do—
invite their guest.

Their guest arrives.
Mice yell, "Surprise!
Happy birthday, old friend,
happy birthday to YOU!"